THE EXPERIMENT STATION

ANDY GARZA

Enzar Empire Press
Gonzalez, Florida
2018

eBook ISBNs:
Kindle: 978-1-63199-503-3
Google Play: 978-1-63199-505-7
iBooks: 978-1-63199-504-0
Aer.io: 978-1-63199-587-3
Kobo: 978-1-63199-588-0

Print:
ISBN: 978-1-63199-502-6

Enzar Empire Press
P. O. Box 841
Gonzalez, FL 32560

https://enzarempire.com

pubs@energion.com

Enzar Empire Press is an imprint of Energion Publications

TABLE OF CONTENTS

1.

Lore, Myths, and Campfire Stories

Lore, myths and campfire stories are all born from fertile seeds of truth. Through the evolutionary track of time newly developed inhabitants of prison earth scrambled for tit-bits of knowledge tossed at them by immigrant settlers from worlds unknown. The immigrants harvested sedimentary dust flying through endless space and formed it into a globe. From the far reaches of the revolving asteroid belt they corralled Neptunian objects of water rich asteroids and guided them to fledgling earth. They needed water in which their creative experiments would take place. Superior to all developing life forms they were the masters of creation. Having forged the universe they took command of all life on the infantile planet as if building and rebuilding the earth would better serve their objective.

From those grains of truth our story begins.

Bigger than life, the screen crackled and buzzed then came alive as members of the chosen committee made themselves comfortable for what could well be a long ordeal. As well known experts they were called in to assess the physical condition of the planet and prescribe possible solutions to the infinite damage affecting it. The reviews were in fact historical visual records and far too many to view and analyze individually and then recommend solutions in the short time allotted. The operators of the screens more or less skimmed through the pages and still presented formidable evidence of the damage in question.

1930. Ambition and greed plowed up more than 150,000 acres for crops thus destroying the root systems of grasses that had long held the land in place. The dry soil became dust and blew across the nation in awesome fury to be dubbed "the black blizzards." The end result was wholesale devastation to an area once teeming with wild life.

1940's. Conflicts for supremacy and territory left huge numbers of innocent people and warriors dead and rotting in the sun. Entire regions in thriving countries were on the brink of total annihilation. Resources and once wholesome ecosystems disrupted for long periods of time. Each episode showed graphic footage of the resulting devastation seemingly worse than the previous one.

1952. During an unexpected cold winter London, England burned tons of coal to keep warm, resulting in huge clouds of hideous black smog to choke the atmosphere. 4,000 lives were reported lost while 100,000 developed respiratory problems for life. No record exists regarding the loss of ecosystems and animal life.

1986. In a remote area of the Ukraine called Chernobyl experiments with nuclear power exploded to release huge amounts of deadly radioactive dust to float across what was then the USSR. Loss of life went undocumented.

1989. The Exxon Valdez oil tanker spill would have a continuing effect for many years to come.

January 2000. Romania received 100,000 cubic meters of toxic water to hold safely behind a dam. (Why, is not clear.) However, the dam failed and 100 tons of cyanide spilled onto productive farm lands on its way to the heavily populated banks of the Danube River, and become a menace to all life forms.

2001. The mercury poisoning in Japan claimed more than 2,265 lives. No record of damage to ecosystems and animal life was accurately kept.

The most recent subject of interest was the numerous sink holes that had materialized in various places around the globe. Even though the phenomena had not caused any known loss of life they were nonetheless on the verge of producing wide spread disasters if such unpredicted indentures continued to grow in size. It was noted that two such sudden pits had occurred in Russia and filled up to become fair sized lakes.

Viewing such awesome devastation urged the travel weary committee to elbow each other and plead for a rest period and some nourishing refreshments. A plea welcomed by all parties. Still to be seen and analyzed was the long list of natural disasters that plagued to planet for eons. Time was required to digest what had been so graphically shown and dwell on some possible solutions. The assignment was an enormous task for even the most brilliant minds. All living forms huge, big, small and microscopic had to be given thoughtful consideration and even the most intelligent minds could not wisp out answers by a flick of their hands. A short impromptu conference was held by leading heads and it was decided that more time was needed to weigh the full scale of the problems. Being of vital importance, it was decided to delve deeper and discover the primary cause of such events. The cause and effect of all this had to have a solid base from which it sprang to such proportions in such a short cosmic period.

After a suitable rest period the committee was not spared the visual records of Rogue waves laying waste to countless shorelines. Bodies of citizens, two legged, four legged or winged bloated and floating on the perilous sea. Then came volcanic eruptions to scorch paths onto living communities and roasting the unwary alive. Giant hurricanes swirling in awesome fury against all living forms and the screen seemed anxious to show the next disaster.

"Enough! That is enough!" the head of the leading assembly almost shouted standing upright with his hands above his head. "We need time to rest from all this and digest it. We must consult our technical directors for aggressive suggestions. We've all known this was happening and for the sake of being honest, I should say that many of us chose to let someone else confront the problems. Well the problems have come to hunt us down, we are pushed against a corner and being so, we will charge into the dilemma and eke out a solution or suitable compromise."

And so the work session was brought to a close. It became time to indulge in some revitalizing refreshment and spend time with old acquaintances and friendly enemies. There was acceptable music filtering in from somewhere and yet from nowhere. Not to mention the countless edible treats and delectable aromas to tempt the more adventuresome appetites. It would take a thick catalogue to itemize each delicious offering. All of which were consumed with notable delight. Not to be forgotten were the needed answers to the primary reason for their presence. They would confront that on their next work period from private as well as open discussions the distinguished assembly formed an approach to the problem. The usual spokes person was unanimously chosen to voice their findings and recommendations.

And so it was that the supreme council of inter-galactic magistrates scheduled a second high level conference at the gigantic hall of justice at an assembly of buildings housing the history of numerous galaxies and developing planets. Not a speck of information was ever left untouched by the keepers of vital records and kept in perfect chronological order. These buildings were not only enormous but were built by long forgotten civilized individuals possessed with great architectural skills and powers of levitation. They represented the solid foundation onto which justice reigned supreme. The scheduled convention was to take place on the long time civil planet of Almira in the distant Galaxy 12 of Voltitmar, 13.1 billion light years from the developing prison earth. Orion's arm was a group of planets within a galaxy known as the Milky Way. On the fringes of that turbulent development the prison planet was formed. Innumerable sites were carefully assigned for arriving council members along with the suitable time of arrival thus avoiding congestion on the landing fields. Vessels of countless shapes and forms were systematically housed in their required atmospheric conditions. Life support systems brought to bear and personal necessities attended to without flaw for council members as well as crew. Proper refreshments, nutritional capsules, liquids or food items all carefully attended to by experts of each necessity. A separate crew of specialists was assigned to the task of maintaining each vessel strange, different or odd to function in perfect order. Identity checks and search for concealed weapons had long been abolished. All vessels were scientifically scanned from great distances and no weapons or false identities had ever eluded the flawless security system. The great halls of justice at Almira had long maintained their integrity with infinite care. The most proper respect and welcome was showered on each arriving council member in admirable order. Each council member had long ago earned the respect of the supreme council by judicial work and contributions made to the unity and welfare of all life forms on the civil planets. Like courtrooms anywhere each individual was required to present themselves in a visual state approved by all. Advanced science had developed chameleon abilities for individuals to use and appear in proper dress code. An attending member could well possess a totally different body but at the courts of Almira all members were transformed into physical appearances acceptable by all. The established system also eliminated possible discrimination which had long ago proven to be an indisputable ally or deterrent to justice being served. Considering all that, much regard was given to the original physical form of council members and which was allowed to show on special occasions.

On the agenda was the fate of all living forms on a tiny developing planet known as earth. The unruly species had violated inter-galactic law, had unlawfully assumed the role of master over that minuscule community and tottered on the brink of destroying all life forms on that celestial body. They were creatures that walked on two legs and chose to call themselves humans. They possessed remarkable evolutionary ability and had the intelligence to progress to a near civilized state. They professed to be respectful to other life forms and benevolent to all. Which was a claim too often proven to be the complete opposite! The planet had developed into a circle of inner species predation. All species lived to feed a greater form of life.

This violation of inter-galactic law was not a first offense. Genes of the biped creatures had been condemned to that tiny developing speck of space debris for similar offenses. Their incarceration on the planet earth was castigation for crimes and devastation rendered to civilizations and inhabitants close to and far beyond Galaxy 12. They had warred without logical reason and master minded the destruction of entire civilizations that opposed their rule. They had developed weapons so powerful as to destroy an entire universe in one stroke, Annihilating all living forms and never damaging valuable properties. They massed duplicated their own kind in laboratory conditions to be brought to war when needed. The council had expected the genes of those aggressive criminals to die off on that savage little earth. They even sent a group of volunteers to form bases and act as wardens of those dangerous felons. They were assigned to witness the demise of those condemned and record it as a sentence duly carried out. Instead of dying off as expected, their genes took a powerful grip onto the spark plug of life at their first opportunity. Not all Guardians of Death adhered faithfully to their given assignments. And some were soon exploring ways to benefit from their genetic prisoners. They launched massive research to gauge the development and present state of their jail. It was considered standard procedure for any warden anywhere to indulge in such a study.

The specks, the spores and the developing microbes that could form the basis of life existed on the land, the created atmosphere and in the newly collected waters of earth. They learned to use cyanobacteria, a blue green algae from whence oxygen emerged to give life to growing species. With unknown necromancy the assigned jailers from distant stars joined the ingredients into a slowly simmering stew until the perfect time. Then without fore knowledge of the end result, randomly released the mixture unto the barren earth. The lifeless planet was fertile soil for the potion of life and played the part of a cocoon from whence countless life forms emerged. The sparkplug and the potion of life joined forces to prove their worth. Without restraint the power of life conquered the winds, occupied every niche of land and mastered the waters with an infinite array of life. The jailers experimented with many living forms and found some not to be in harmony with the juvenile planet. Others were of the self-destruct variety and so the incarcerated gene wove its way cautiously through the melee of perilous creation. From those horrifying and humble beginnings the condemned gene gathered food for its survival and development. Should it live through the destruction and turbulence of the world around it? Father time, the ultimate supervisor of all development would coordinate the future paths on which the condemned gene would travel and to what destination. A destination too distant and forbidden to contemplate, since the juvenile planet was not a simple follow the blue print endeavor in jig saw fashion. There were peaks and pitfalls that even the most learned jailer could not foresee.

FROM THE RUBBLE OF CONSTRUCTION

The Guardians of Death were accused of intervening and disrupting the natural evolutionary process of those earthly beings by intoxicating their primitive minds with promises of grandeur. It was said they made kings of some and slaves of others while openly copulating with their females. Therefore the Guardians of Death were also on trial. The supreme council would discuss and review the complexity of these allegations many times before arriving at a just and fair conclusion. Were the Guardians of Death totally guilty of manipulating the course of the condemned and evolving human species? Or was the human gene not worth the effort it took to save their kind, since they had proven untrustworthy before? Their violations on distant planets long ago followed a similar pattern of behavior as shown on recent reports. They were self destructive, power hungry, unruly savages with no regard for their own future.

The Guardians of Death were on trial for yet a more serious offense. Their historical records proved that it was they that chose the isolated location to create the infant planet for the incarceration of the human type gene. They were suspected of choosing earth's location for reasons of their own, not yet known. The Guardians of Death had volunteered to serve as the wardens of that secret location. Colossal eruptions, climatic convulsions, liquids pouring from the blackened skies for long periods added to the drama of creation. Hell fire blasting from the heavens helped stir the ever simmering pot of genesis. Then came an ever changing parade of land, air and sea creatures that challenged the struggling human species. Land carnivores roamed the earth in awesome size and numbers. Looking, always looking for warm blooded flesh for sustenance and the hunt included the tender developing human species.

However, whether by plan or natural cause a giant asteroid collided with the struggling earth and destroyed the support systems of large carnivores. Resulting in a frozen world spinning in isolation and total darkness for eons of time. The waters of the world froze to a near complete globe of Ice, miles thick in some areas. The prisoners of the planet were sure to be obliterated in an icy environment with little or no warn sunlight. It was expected that the outlaw gene would die off in that turbulent and microbial infested construction site. But when the smoke and debris from the process of development finally settled, the phoenix of humanity, the genes embedded in ice managed to rise from the ashes and the dust. They survived on rancid meat and bones left on the fields of slaughter by nature or prowling carnivores. To overcome their perilous stage of existence they became scavengers competing with violent beasts for leftovers and other decaying matter.

Barely crawling from pains, illness and hunger man continued a near starving existence. Therein the law of survival stepped forth to lend a strong arm to the struggling, infant genus homos and increase their numbers. They went into the field and multiplied among their own kind and other migrating manlike species. It was a reproduction process that sparked the curiosity of the Wardens. The Guardians of Death assigned to witness the demise of the outlaw gene and record it as a sentence duly carried out were awe struck by the determination of their prisoners to survive such enormous obstacles. Current data to the courts of Almira recorded the survival, but not in infinite detail. The gamogenesis process of these primitive beings required careful scientific study before a full report was rendered. Earth was well hidden behind and far beyond the exploding barriers of galactic development. Stars were becoming novas; black holes were sucking up entire planets with the most powerful force in all the known universe and galaxies. An infinite ocean of destruction and rebuilding was taking place making this deep space simmering pot uninhabitable to civil life. Once leaving the prison planet, there was a dark and frigid ocean of emptiness. Few if any star charts existed at the civil planets to guide expeditions to the tiny earth. And so it remained a carefully guarded secret that added permanent security to the prison of the outlaw gene. It was in fact, an effective barrier that served well as the prison walls of those kept therein. The disruptive human gene would fight hard of eons of time to overpower their confinement without outside intervention. While the lure from the stars never ceased to be a nightly vigil to his insatiable curiosity.

In a short period of galactic time man borrowed or stole knowledge from his keepers and was developing into a free thinking species. Man became capable of deep thoughts and able to cipher on deep complicated problems that lay on his path of progress. For all that, humanity deserved credit worth considering by the supreme council. Reports to the home planet indicated that the progressive human was close to reinventing himself by genetic duplication. Already he could duplicate animals from a test tube in the laboratory. He was experimenting with becoming a self functioning, self sustaining machine. A man like machine developed from computerized elements to self upgrade as new components came to use. Not a single substance of the living human was overlooked. Every minuscule contributing part was carefully duplicated to greatly outperform the living tissue. The improved human with all parts intact would be covered over by a stronger and more durable human like skin. The living flesh had proven weak and unreliable as it grew old. Therefore it was expedient to discard the original living flesh in lieu of a stronger more durable material. With new found knowledge on the workings of genetic materials humans could create a man and or woman in laboratory conditions. It could be possible for the new synthetic human in the proper traveling vessel to find its way back to their former home. An initial point that could be summed up with studious exploration of their genes' origins. Knowing not where that journey would take them or if it would ever come to pass. For the present, their experiments with genetic duplication were simply toys to exercise the mind. But nonetheless explore future possibilities. These very facts posed a considerable threat to civility, the Guardians of Death must prevent.

Credit would also be considered by the council on the primitive human's efforts to adjust to their early confinement. To overcome the enormous obstacles posed by an ever volatile planet without advanced protection and habitation. Through sheer determination they had overcome the colossal power of a changing earth. Humans ran the obstacle course of evolution tirelessly for eons. He lived in fear of the night, shivering in cold caves and near starvation. His kind was often consumed by his predator neighbors in the early light of day. He suffered countless injuries without medical attention and only his will to survive as his aide in arms. He had done arduous penance for his forbearer's crimes. He finally learned to deal with fire and to use local materials to make tools and weapons with which to hunt and provide food for his family and himself. He learned to cover his puny body with the skins taken from the animals he hunted and by so doing inherited the animal's parasites unto himself.

However, the warrior element within the incarcerated gene that annihilated countless worlds before now had yet to accept peaceful co-existence. The warrior element lived within the developing species and so man would wield the ax of power for eons before he addressed his issues at a conference table. That revelation was not properly addressed at the courts of Almira.

3.

THE PRICE OF PROGRESS

Later the tools he forged became weapons to protect his homeland and food supply. Still later to gain new hunting grounds, from there he learned invasion and to make war on his neighbors for power and territory. The ax of power gained its place in the hand of man. Soon thereafter man progressed on multiple veins of achievement. He remained power hungry, always in quest for greater knowledge. He suffered near starvation, injuries and confinement in caves for safety. When ample food and territory became secure man knew not the meaning of enough. He would grab and fight for more than he could hold for a long time before he learned the laws of civil restraint. He remained always drawn to study the heavens above him forever searching for what, he did not know. In summation, man comprised a remarkable story of survival, had he done it on his own. All this and more would be considered by the judicial council.

The Guardians of Death were charged with manipulating the human gene for their own purposes. In the safety of total isolation the primitive human could be tactfully programmed to behave in controlled ways. The Wardens of human confinement were in full command of utilizing their prisoners as they saw best fit their needs. Sources of energy were becoming more difficult to obtain, more costly to produce as well as transport. But on earth the energy sources were boundless. They were forbidden to use the resources designated for the development of planet earth and its inhabitants and so they didn't, to a degree. They discovered a remarkable self generating source of energy untapped ever before. Man with his ever growing numbers was an amazing reservoir of power. The force within the human mind could be captured at the time of his demise and transferred into fuel cells. It was then used to power in board environments, energize equipment, computers, control panels, lights and multiple other needs. Energy for propulsion was spared the burden of ship board requirements. The drummed up reports read that the planet was unsafe for civil life forms since humans were always on the defensive and tended to attack intruders in their territories without warning. Civil citizens were forbidden to retaliate against lower life forms therefore they avoided earth with serious regard. When in reality the Guardians of Death were safeguarding a valuable power source. In so doing they also concealed the method by which that power source was acquired. The Guardians of Death were alleged to have instigated numerous wars, masterminded deadly accidents and climatic disruptions solely to harvest the power within the human brain. A brain that was in effect a computer of living flesh programmed to perform specific functions. Then kept productive in synthetic conditions to traverse the heavens in shipboard comfort. The process of capturing the human brain power was a simple matter of net and catches with the skillful use of proper tools. The storage of the secret power cells was a more complex endeavor, requiring uncanny skill and precise timing. Since this was a widely known criminal offense, the secrets of this undertaking was a highly guarded process. Only those in the innermost circles of secrecy knew the correct procedure and in due course passed it on to trusted conspirators. Should the allegations reported to the supreme council prove true, the crimes would multiply in seriousness?

An account would be taken of the human lives lost to the Guardians of Death manipulations since it constituted premeditation and completion of open criminal offenses. The Wardens of Earth were at a perilous point in their careers. It could result in severing their span of existence. To interfere in the life process of other living beings was a crime punishable by expulsion from the civil planets with all rights denied, very little survival gear and life sustaining supplies. A penalty humans were still suffering. The infested planet was off limits to all civil life forms, primarily due to influence by the Guardians of Death. Earth, the created planet was known to harbor an immense array of self sustaining life. The sparkplug of creation had been studiously modified to empower all life forms on prison earth. It was a production formula enviable by other distant civilizations.

The civil planets of Voltimar were free of illness or threatening life forms. They were sterilized at birth and immunized against all health and life threatening hazards. New wardens would be secured and prepared for the multiple hazards of earth, while the incarcerated humans went to trial. Man was charged with the destructive use of their prison. The mutilation and annihilation of many living species and gross contamination of their life support systems. Man had dangerously polluted the waters on earth with the debris of his progress; the skies were filthy with his own emissions. Their insatiable greed for fuels stored within the earth were endangering large portions of the earth's delicate crust to collapse unto itself causing huge sink holes that could swallow a continent. Humanity had become a cancer on the earth with no foreseeable means of restoring what they destroyed. Although they were condemned to the infantile earth, they had nonetheless been provided with all the essentials needed to develop into an acceptable civil form of life. Humans alone or with outside help had profaned the mandates of civil order and stood on trial for their disrespect of inter-galactic law.

The Guardians of Death were no doubt partly to blame. The question before the supreme council was how much manipulation had the Wardens of prison earth used on the struggling primitive man? How guilty were the Guardians of Death for man's disruptive comportment? And who would defend man at the highest tribunal of inter-planetary justice? From what civil planet would a qualified attorney be found to even consider the case, which was literally open and shut? Man was guilty. There was no need to gather volumes of evidence. Vintage and current films with scientific documentation were available at the push of a button for all to examine. Man was guilty. Plain and simple. Their crimes were far more than simple vandalism.

In a stumbling, fumbling fashion man struggled to attain all the knowledge required to prevent his earthly condition and he ignored the devastation of his creation in lieu of his self proclaimed greatness. A fact he could not deny before the massive evidence against him.

In an effort to save the human gene the supreme council voted to go a step further and implement specific rules of behavior to the unruly human and put a stop to their uncivil insanity. Widen the portals of knowledge and nudge man to evolve into a more civil species. They had survived their initial ordeal and appeared worthy of considering their reacceptance into civil order. Teach man to use justice, the rules of righteousness and how to exist in peace with his neighbors. It was an added assignment for the duty weary Wardens of Earth. However, that grant of new power was soon abused by the Guardians. It was suspected they were guilty of assuming an unauthorized life form, greater in size than the largest living human, stronger and of course more intelligent. They were titans and presented themselves as celestial beings from distant stars. The puny human species cowered and bowed before the giants that walked the earth as though they owned it.

Not long after the Guardians of Death grew overly fond of the adoration bestowed upon them. They cherished being exalted by the puny, primitive man creatures in their keep. The worship became an intoxicating elixir of individual greatness which they consumed with feverish hunger. Some Guardians grossly violated the primary civil law by destroying other guards within their ranks to attain the ultimate greatness. The fall of a guardian by whatever means left all his belonging up for grabs by other Guardians. It was a lesson humans would painfully carry far into their future. Battles among the titans were awesome displays of power the puny human witnessed. Man was then easily coerced to obey without question the god like survivors. They were often sentenced to serve the Wardens for minor offenses and many were enslaved without release to fulfill the growing demands of the Guardians of Death. Great buildings were constructed to honor the victors of recent struggles, also to provide luxurious homes for them. Temples were erected to worship these superior beings. Humanity learned architecture and construction the hard way; they learned it under threat of punishment and by enslaved labor. Extra care was taken by the Guardians to spread their knowledge and skills among the more intelligent humans and keep the less brilliant as the labor force. As forced laborers they built temples, halls of justice and homes for the Wardens growing needs of administrative staffs. All this while they dwelled in luxury at the expense of human sweat. They made kings from among the humans and subdivided their habitats into controllable plots of territory.

While the harvesting of human brain power never ceased. Humans had become like ripened fruit to be harvested in due time. The Guardians of Death had become nothing less than a common thief, stealing precious life time from helpless humans. He became an assassin for his own gain. Man was helpless to ward off the manipulations of his keepers and was systematically coerced to war against his neighbors. The harvest of brain power would fill countless fuel canisters after each human encounter on the battle fields. The human flesh then became a useless shell to be devoured by scavengers, incinerated or promptly buried for fear of wide spread contamination. To which the Guardians of Death were not totally immune. They carefully guarded against exposure to such decaying matter and infected environments. Were they to fall victims of their own folly, they would lose their superiority before the eyes of their adoring humans.

Countless scientific expeditions from Voltimar's civil planets and beyond were known to visit the blue globe on occasion. They came to do research on the human progress, to check atmospheric conditions which were known to exist nowhere else and even abduct humans for scientific investigation. To perform medical checks so to speak. Man had developed into a remarkable species. Visitors collected samples of all living matter for further study in home laboratories. Before any of this could happen, it was required to secure permission to enter the prison planet from the Guardians of Death. Permission not easily granted by the Wardens of detention center earth. Therefore, each visit from the civil planets was closely monitored by the jail keepers and was in most cases a pushed and rushed affair. Contamination from the infinite sources in the earthly environment could cause serious damage to homebound ships traveling through uncharted space. The matter generated genuine concern from all parties involved. A home bound ship could leave a trail of harmful microbes in their wake. Members of such expeditions were in equal danger, although countless precautions were always taken. Protective gear was in constant use and decontamination chambers were kept ready to purify returning members of such expeditions. A Single earth born germ could have devastating effects on the sterile planets of Galaxy 12. The end result of these hurried and monitored visits protected the secrets kept by the Guardians of Death. And so the clandestine activities of the celestial beings from distant stars continued non-stop. While man was not able to suspect the tiniest sliver of such heinous endeavors.

A surprising discovery gained wide attention from the Wardens and distillers of human brain power. It had been scientifically proven that the wicked, degenerate, criminally motivated human mind was not as reliable and productive as the power gathered from the more intelligent and righteous beings. Therefore it was mandated without recourse to dispose of the unacceptable grade brain power by incineration. There to burn for eternity until not even the ashes existed. While the higher grades of brain energy were cultivated in shipboard comfort to produce more favorable results.

But not all human deaths were recorded and collected for distillation. Many lives were lost to accidents or natural causes in the wilderness or inaccessible places and escaped being milled into power cells. Another startling development arose to awareness by those keenly interested in the power within the human mind. It became a full time study for the scientific community within the Guardians of Death. They discovered that some human minds were able to defeat death and re-emerge in the body of a new born child. The scientists were challenged to discover how this amazing feat of survival was done. Could it be a practiced exercise that one could do while still in the aging stage of their current existence? Leaders and beings of supreme importance would be very interested in learning the secrets of this phenomenon so they could live forever in new revitalized bodies. Their minds would never die. The capricious grip on life by the human gene could survive death many times over as well. But, they were seemingly content to remember countless events from their previous existence with remarkable accuracy. They gave thought or expressed gratitude for reincarnating into a new life. While the scientist dug deep into the amazing feat by such a primitive life form as the developing human. It was even somewhat degrading. Being they were such advanced and intelligent beings. Conclusive answers to the bewildering feat escaped even the most inquisitive researcher. The human gene had simply found another way to overcome death. The will to survive, the capriciousness of the human gene gained long overdue admiration and perhaps a shaded respect from the Wardens. While they relentlessly pursued the obvious question. How did the human mind achieve such an extraordinary ability? For lack of a conclusive answer it was labeled a Source of Unexplained Life, then filed away to be forgotten. Humans would later learn to call this phenomenon Reincarnation. There was much else that always demanded the attention of the studious galactic scientist. The developing world was an enormous study room.

The Guardians became enraptured on many occasions by the physical beauty the human female had attained over time. She had progressed from a tangled hair, filth encrusted, and insect infested, malodorous woman into a smooth skinned and extremely alluring female. Having little to wear she innocently paraded in a near nude state. Until she learned that her physical attributes were in demand and exploited every means of improving what she had. The jailers of earth became equally captivated by the human female's willingness to copulate with them. Copulation as humans knew it had not been practiced on the civil planet for eons of time. Therefore to indulge in the act of actual fornication was in effect, a new experience for the Wardens of death. An experience that required practice to prolong into mutual satisfaction. It was nonetheless an open violation of their given assignment and so recorded. The Guardians marveled endlessly at the physical pleasure from freely copulating with a human female. It was a pleasure long forgotten in their history.

Reproduction of their own kind had been reduced to a purely scientific procedure in their home planets. Their behavior was in open violation of their assignment. So great was the attraction to both sexes that intercourse with more than one member of the opposite gender became common practice. Frightful numbers of half breed humans grew up never knowing who their fathers were. A select few Wardens deemed this behavior as regressing from their superior state to the level of wild animals responding to a programmed biological estrus. At the courts of Almira this activity would go on file as "serious infractions noted" then to the initials S.I.N.

The select few that refused to participate in such ancient and degrading rituals of reproduction were adhering to their original assignments. Humans were still near savage animals. Inmates in their keep and to ensnare them into illegal activities such as sexual indulgence were strictly forbidden by the supreme council. Equally ensnared were the Guardians that found the new sensations long forgotten vastly intriguing and were not able to tear themselves away from the activity of a beastly rut. And so both sexes were victims of powerful biological forces beyond their strength or willingness to ignore. Some Guardians could not understand the attraction. It was not rational to feel an attraction this powerful for a near animal being. The activity blatantly disregarded the orders of their assignment. It disobeyed the supreme council's dictate of non interference. It abandoned the civil laws of righteousness. It was open rebellion against their advanced concepts of a refined civil life.

It was some time before they rediscovered and accepted the word, love. The discovery stirred new sensations within the less sated jailers of earth. Even more overwhelming was the sight of their offspring coming to life from within the bowels of a human female. In countless instances the child came forth with strong resemblances to the father in miniature form. To the Wardens this was an awe inspiring occurrence they would not soon forget. They resumed the deep care for mother and child that laid dormant in the back corridors of their minds from time unknown. They were learning to love again and the habit grew stronger with time.

Being that the warden's tenure on earth would be a long assignment, some were allowed to bring their life mates and offspring and live their family life styles in protected but nonetheless primitive conditions. It would be safe to say that the adventure of living in such crude environments would generate stories for their future families to hear. Young daughters born of celestial beings found charm and were fascinated beyond restraint by the progressive but still somewhat savage human males and fornicated with them. Wives having long existed in a near sexless state were equally enthralled by the exhilarating sensations that sex on earth produced and many indulged in that forbidden pleasure. These secret rendezvous and public relationships became the core material for countless legends and love stories recounted many times before man learned to write. Man's keen imagination learned to inflate these stories to please the listener and deflate them when needed. By close association with these celestial beings now firmly embedded and calling earth their home, man was experiencing a giant intellectual leap forward. During all this, humans made many efforts to thwart the warden's abusiveness by force. Wardens had become overly wanton in their quest of sexual pleasure and too often abducted desirable human females at will. From those efforts humans learned to honor their fallen heroes with dignity and respect at burials or incinerations.

The Wardens of Earth became more powerful from human adoration. They seemed to draw strength from exaltation and to prove humanity's sincerity, the Wardens demanded tribute in the form of food and gold, a share of the harvest, woven materials and temporary keep of human vestal virgins. They were self inflated with greatness and chose to forget their original purpose on earth. They plotted to keep earth as their own and rise from a glorified but lowly zoo keeper to being master of the world and the puny human race as their subjects. They comprised a powerful force securely kept behind dangerous star barriers in a secret corner of an expanding universe. The energy from human brains was slowly reinvented to use in destructive weapons even they, were not able to gauge.

4.

DISSENSION AMONG THE GODS

Man was still in the infantile stages of mental development and not able to brand the Guardians of Death as being a God, since the word or meaning of "God" was yet to exist. Adoration stemmed purely from the physical strength and deeds of these celestial immigrants.

Although all Guardians of Death were adored for their greatness they all fell into the category of supreme beings, notable dissension existed among them. There were those that seriously opposed copulation with lower life forms. Others believing the rumors were true, insisted on abandoning the harvesting of human brain power as being felonious crimes that would draw severe punishment were it true and known by the supreme council. These righteous groups joined to turn the wrong doers back into the path of their original assignment. A task not easily accomplished. And so for this reason and others too numerous to mention, battles among the Wardens of death broke out throughout the heavens and earth as well. The Wardens fought and many fell like boulders from the sky. After many diplomatic conferences, a truce was declared. And while the terms of a permanent peace were worked out, fragile tranquility returned to earth. They hid their sexual aggressions more effectively. They strengthened their security systems to better protect the brain power project. The more glory hungry stood firm on their illegal activities. They had deemed earth a place to breed discontent to cultivate then reap human brain energy for their own use. To copulate with earth women was a simple matter of taking what they wanted and when they wanted it. They collected females and housed them to use and enjoy at their leisure. Their harems were a place where the most attractive and talented women were housed in enviable comfort. With no interference from anybody since no human male was strong or wise enough to oppose them. Females from all social classes of human life adored their new found status. They were now consorts, mistresses, advisors and even wives to these powerful citizens from distant stars. Chosen females were cherished as supreme beings alongside their celestial mates. They grew by deed, talent or beauty alone to be adored by their previous kind. In short, they were exalted to the status of women of superior charm and excellence. The status elevation, the luxurious way of life and the adoration they received was a tonic too powerful to refuse. They could not live in caves and hovels anymore. These choice women found a way to survive and leave behind their former caste. It was Mother Nature's way of improving the species in her keep. From all this future generations took another step forward in the drama of human progress.

Peace treaties were broken, agreements were distorted to discontent and arguments took precedence among the Guardians of Death. As a peaceful adjustment, sporting competitions became prevalent as they challenged each other for dominance while a helpless human race could only look on. These friendly competitions did not stop at being simple games for a higher score; they went beyond the playing fields to become deadly conflicts. They soon escalated to open warfare again. Many Guardians met their demise and promptly become fodder for the brain fuel cell campaign silently and meticulously carried out in improved secret conditions. The human mind was quickly learning to keep records, to add figures, to formulate plans and taking lessons from their celestial captors rise above an incarcerated breed. They longed for freedom from the tyranny of celestial beings and that quest would follow them into the distant future. Humans adored the physical strength and intellect of their keepers and strove relentlessly to achieve a degree of it for themselves. The portals of knowledge opened a bit wider and the inquisitive mind of man took another leap forward. The multiple activities of the Guardians became precious keepsakes for man as his intellect grew; he recorded every incident minor or major for future generations. The love affairs, their battles, the schemes within schemes and daily activities went from truth to campfire stories to myths or legends not soon forgotten. Never knowing that in so doing they were writing an arrest warrant for the Guardians of Death. Countless true to life files of guardian activity found their way to the supreme council at Almira. Council members and superior judges were appalled at the Wardens' maladministration of their assignment. They immediately summoned all council members to Voltimar to join in a discussion and devise a proper plan of action against the Guardians. Their malfeasance of office must stop immediately. Should the reports and rumors be true? Until proven without doubt, they were simply rumors invented by the mischievous developing humans. And there it remained without proof in hand. The Wardens were all honorable beings and the charges against them were no doubt false.

Earth had become similar to a pasture where prime livestock was raised. Breeding and interbreeding their human specimens celestial beings continued to improve their customized toys to produce a more effective brain power, while not ignoring the pleasures human females provided. The warring Guardians were annihilating themselves in heroic individual battles as well as encounters across the skies before the bewildered eyes of humans. Fallen Wardens were often written about as admirable heroes defending their sense of righteousness. Many of those so called fallen heroes were Wardens that opposed the illegal activities of the power hungry guardian outlaws.

Those power hungry Guardians had resolved to fight for their dominance of earth and would do battle with the supreme council's army using earth as a battle field, if need be. The result would be a catastrophe earth could not withstand without regressing to the infant days of the planet. The power hungry Guardians had acquired loved ones and families and were near acclimated to the environmental conditions. Earth was a paradise of opportunity. It was a real place of never ceasing marvels. No doubt, the mighty titans were falling in love with the wonders of their creation. All living things were finding comfort in the atmosphere developing throughout. With medical adjustments the Wardens learned to breathe the life sustaining gases of earth and flourished with them. They grew fond of the exhilarating sensations coursing through their bodies and instilling the joy of life. They would not easily relinquish their grip on earth. But some of the mighty titans were falling from old age, not adjusting to environmental gases, contracted diseases, infestations by minute organisms prevalent on earth. All of which were unforeseen events by the highly sanitized and immunized celestial beings from distant stars. As Guardians fell, their life's accomplishments and activities were recorded by the scribes and story tellers among the human lot. They became glorified heroes of truth and or fiction and their names awarded to heavenly bodies as the ultimate reverence to their origin and their deeds. A righteous guardian known for his knowledge and experience in matters of war was given his name to the red planet Mars. The mighty Jupiter soon joined him in a heavenly berth and Venus was allotted favor for her charm and beauty. An unnamed body of water got its name from the God, Atlas. Atlantic Ocean. Lastly and no less honorably Saturn, the mentor of agriculture when peace came about was granted his heavenly honor.

5.

In a Fertile Valley Far Away

At the informal discussions, highly fictitious stories drifted into loosely given attention. It was fantasized that in a fertile valley on earth were three rivers flowed, fruits and edible vegetables along with berries also seeds and nuts existed in abundance. Creatures of many kinds seemed to live in harmony in this enviable and enchanted valley. It was suggested by way of implication that it was in this place somewhere around the waist of the world, that the Wardens of Earth committed their most felonious transgression. It was a place vested with miracles now lost in the faded pages of time. Within this long lost paradise by scientific and medical manipulation modern man and woman saw their first days on earth as homogeneous beings. They were comprised in part by elements from the Wardens of Earth and the more advanced indigenous creatures. The over whelming results astonished even the most advanced scientific minds of the Guardians of Death. They knew well what they had created and chose to keep the secret to themselves. To side step suspicion their records labeled the end result as natural evolution like so many other living forms were doing. They preferred to believe that they had given the incarcerated outlaw gene a new beginning and installed it in a new body. However grand the accomplishment was, it was nonetheless strictly forbidden to interfere, let alone manipulate species of other worlds. And the Guardians of Death had known it well.

First and foremost were the proven transgressions of the inmates of planet earth. Though the stories regarding the Wardens of Earth were disturbing, they were nonetheless unproven and regarded as baseless rumors. Humans were yet to be granted credit for thinking, ciphering and planning ahead by the supreme council too far away to know the truth. The Wardens of death had been carefully selected to perform their given assignment with honor. It was concluded after long debate that the dual problems would be addressed in sequence. Therefore the supreme council decided to dispatch a qualified search team to find on earth a man, perhaps two men that would best represent the human race at the preliminary hearing on Almira.

On earthbound Tibet, a holy man was found with superior intelligence, vast world knowledge and learned in the workings of law and justice. While within the religious domain of Rome in Italia, a second man of equal intelligence was chosen. These men would answer the charges brought against the human race. Once an inter-galactic attorney was secured to defend them and all other prerequisites were properly attended. The earth men would simply be abducted and transported to the trial site, completely unharmed. In fact, the procedure was so swift that the men would ponder for many earth years what really happened. While the Guardians of Death were ordered to appear in court at a given time with no options granted. Their legal summons was abbreviated to GOD. Their summons was addressed as G.O.D. Location: Earth station **1**. The word God had never been used on the advanced civil planets. On this occasion it was nothing more than a legal abbreviation. Henceforth at their investigative hearings the Wardens of prison earth would be addressed and known as GOD plus their individual identification numbers. The options were simple; refusing to appear in court would be considered an admission of guilt. The armies of Galaxy 12 would then come to take the Guardians of Death by force. War would no doubt ensue causing vast devastation to an already fragile planet. Another fact to consider was that the Wardens of Earth were dying off. They passed on a few at a time from conflicts among themselves. The earthly gases and bacterial infections were taking the greater toll on the almighty titans. Although their numbers had dwindled, they still presented a respectable force not to be taken lightly. Only the most headstrong and hardy individuals managed to overcome the environmental difficulties and remain in battle form.

Secondly and more logical was to appear as the summons requested and coach their attorneys on how to best defend their careless undertaking by showing how the earthly beings had advanced so rapidly and had become more civil-conscious. How their remarkable beauty was so far advanced from their beginnings. Elaborate the fact that the human gene originated from an already intelligent being and therefore not a great obstacle to develop into a secondary intelligent species. Expound the gene's enormous fortitude to overcome such monstrous obstacles and therefore place no surprising wonder that they had achieved their current status so quickly. The Guardians of Death agreed to plead guilty to the charge of manipulation. They addressed the issue as simply making an effort to help the fledgling human race become more law abiding and acceptable into the realm of civil order. Most importantly was to keep the milling of human brain power out of the agenda. The Wardens of Earth would expend much time and spare no effort to completely obscure all incriminating evidence of such activity. It would be very difficult to prove them guilty of such a heinous endeavor. To that charge, they would plead not guilty and remain steadfast until proven otherwise. The GOD would put forth tremendous effort to highlight their favorable deeds and prove their efforts worthy of recognition and even praise. They would work equally hard to keep their post on earth. For they so loveth the earth; they preferred it to any other planet close to or beyond Galaxy 12. For a time they glorified the sunrise and sunset as marvelous creations of life, knowing full well that it was nothing more than a scientific occurrence. But men would accept it as a gift from the Masters of creation on earth as well as heaven and live with that implanted idea until time immemorial. The Guardians would praise the swells of the oceans and all that lived within. No living species on earth was left untouched by their inquisitive tentacles. Everything they explored became a new path to greater knowledge. Such accurate record keeping would prove useful at their Almira trial. They were protectors of all lesser life forms and their field studies proved it. Their behavior in darkened rooms were simply rumors. By definition they were conforming to their assignment. Without being reminded, the atmospheric gases and conditions on earth were killing them. But it was a worthwhile penalty. Their scientists put forth greater effort to find a solution to the problems since it affected them as well. They strove relentlessly to perfect a solution and thus remain young and masters over mankind for infinite time. They grew even more cautious over their illegal activities and spread throughout the earth to create new civilizations. In due process they garnished the muscle power of mankind to build giant temples that always pointed to the infinity of space. They were keeping an ever watchful eye for investigating expeditions from Voltimar's civil planets. The temples also gave humans a specific place to worship their celestial jailers. There was power to be garnished from concentrated adoration. It became a worship from which they drew exhilarating pleasure beyond logical understanding. It was human brain power in a different form. They urged mankind to build statues in their likeness, always striving to have portraits of themselves be greater than those of other Wardens. While the mind of man was so well coerced as to have no alternative but to comply and worship these beings from faraway stars. The Guardians of Death had attained an adoration that would pass through countless generations for earthly centuries to come. Their existence became the creed of humanity all over the world. They were Gods and their word was undisputed law. The worship of these celestial beings gave birth to the word religion. But some men perceived these beings in different ways. The stories of their glory often changed by compass direction. Slowly but surely religion grew into an intangible commodity used by unscrupulous men that saw profit in plain sight. Although religion served as a harness on man's unruliness, it was regarded as too unproductive an effort by the societies beyond Galaxy 12. It was not worth considering in view of the lawlessness so openly practiced. The Guardians of Death would argue that using religion was an effort to draw the lawless human closer to the council's approval. While agreeing they produced a small favorable result, they argued that their efforts were notable and deserved credit. They pleaded with the council to grant them more time to continue their indoctrination of man onto a path of civility by religious means. While man on earth continued his reckless and destructive ways.

Never in the memory or the records kept by primitive man had so many strange objects traversed the earthly skies. Vessels of countless shapes and forms became a common occurrence. Some even landed and made their bodily forms known to the fear ridden population. The fledgling human perceived the incidents as God coming to earth from heaven. Many humans looked forward to Godly visits for eons of time and predicted their return. The celestial beings remained always careful to maintain a safe distance from the infestations of mankind. It appeared their curiosity towards man was shared equally by the inquisitive, braver humans. The more artful human found ways to record these events by crude sketches, paintings, primitive sculptures and word descriptions. No where on earth had these celestial visitors not been seen by the keen human eye.

Man again took an unrestrained leap into the uncertain future. It was an unprecedented leap far beyond the expectations of the engineers of the prison planet. Man found ways to convert his isolated penitentiary into a working planet. He became a working prisoner in his own home. Earth was no longer a spit of left over spacedust, it was a world beaming with life and infinite wonder. Man was struggling to overcome his devastation of natural resources. As mandated he went into the world to become fruitful and fill the earth. And that included his efforts to develop a new synthetic human to withstand the perils of time and climatic changes mostly caused by his own progress. It was labeled cloning. It was first intended for therapeutic purposes but soon whetted the scientific possibility of duplicating a customized man.

Man had been like a battery operated toy for the law breaking Guardians of Death. When the battery ran out of power, there were very few ways to restore it and so men died. It was no great loss since the deceased became fuel for the brain power cell project. While righteous Guardians simply looked on.

Opposition continued between the Guardians as their numbers dwindled. Those in favor of continuing brain cell harvesting and the manipulation of humanity's evolution were regarded as the Violators of Life Systems by the group that adhered firmly to their initial assignment. They were originally sent to witness the demise of an outlaw gene as a sentence duly carried out. But such had not been the case. The condemned gene dug deep into his inner self and survived his death sentence with a degree of admiration. Some Guardians of Death saw this turn of events as time to give up their assignment and return to the civil planets. But their sense of righteousness could not allow them to leave the violators of life systems in command of earth. They were obligated to carry out their most recent task of teaching man the use of justice and civil righteousness. It was a program that continued at a very slow pace. Man held firm to the lessons left behind by the Wardens of Earth. They took what they wanted any way they could and so conquerors and invaders would long postpone civic order within the ranks of man. Conflicts between humans would color the pages of countless lifetimes in glowing crimson before law and order would take a faltering grip. Such conflicts kept the distillers of human brain power extremely busy, considering their efforts had to be super-secrets, carried out by night. They were seen as grotesque figures dressed in black and waving their harvesting tools at corpses like a blessing wand.

Those GOD that held fast to their initial assignment fortified their numbers and strengthened their resolve to see their commission to the end. Man could well terminate his existence by his own carelessness at any given moment. Should that ominous expectation become reality the Guardians of Death would have fulfilled their obligation honorably and return to the civil planets. While still on earth they would continue to bring law and order to the misguided mind of man. They were righteous beings and their assignment was an endeavor of honor. They gained their guidance from other heavenly father figures inhabiting the civil planets far beyond. Those Wardens that capriciously hung on to their wanton ways were now labeled "the Violators of Life Systems." They joyfully fornicated their way through the pages of human history. Some were said to have copulated with animals and became campfire stories about half animal half human beings roaming the earth for centuries. One such creature was named Pan; he was half man half goat and played a flute exquisitely inviting men to come party with him. Another such creature was half horse half man, called Centaur. The harvesting of human brain power still went on in top secret conditions. It was believed that the violators of life had found a profitable market for their illicit merchandise somewhere in the immensity of space. Humanity became a fox eat fox game for the Violators of life systems to play like humans would one day learn to play chess. Humans were used as chess pieces with no qualms. They could be coerced to multiply in masses, manipulated into pointless wars and were doing well at destroying their own kind with their carelessness. An event the Guardians were in no hurry to prevent. It was too rich an opportunity and they could not be blamed for the folly of mankind.

Earth born *Homo sapiens* could not exist in the controlled environments of a space ship. Two earth men were on board a ship going to the planet Almira. Their accommodations were adjusted to their physical needs since they were unaccustomed to a totally microbial free atmosphere. Artificial gravity kept them walking upright, although they never knew the complexity of their detainment. They were encapsulated within an invisible globe that provided them with air to breathe and kept their body temperatures in perfect accord to their requirements. Although not needed, food capsules and fresh water was available for their convenience. And not surprising fresh clothes, under garments and footwear along with personal hygiene items were all neatly packed and within reach.

Anil of Tibet (Air and wind) stood to be introduced to the supreme council of Almira and answer the charges against mankind. A humble looking earth man, short in stature with brown intelligent looking eyes and hair not fully gray yet. He conveyed himself in short calculated strides as though time would last forever. His demeanor transmitted a certain self confidence and he demonstrated no fear of where he was or why he was there. Like any creature of notable intelligence he was caught staring at some of the strange individuals that surrounded him. Equally so, he felt scrutinized in return. He had been properly instructed by various tutors and translators regarding the severity of the charges against earth men. His defending attorneys listened intently to his every translated word brought to them through tiny microphones attached to their hearing appendages. While all spoken matter was properly recorded. Anil of Tibet took notice that the documents before him were written in the Tibetan language. He looked puzzled at his defending team, drawing a simple answer. "We've done all we know to make sure you fully understand the severity of this trial and the future of your kind on earth." With childish curiosity a defending attorney made a curious inquiry, "Setting this case aside and while we have time, we would like to know if it is true that on earth your females squirt out their infants from within their bellies?" And the question was asked with genuine regard and curiosity as though it was impossible for that to happen. Disbelief resonated from their inquiry bringing mild laughter from Anil of Tibet. "We humans have not found a way we like better to produce our young. And "Yes" our females eject a newborn child from within their bodies and produce a new life." Glances of disbelief flashed across the faces of Anil's defending team. Such gruesome comportment was unthinkable. It was unsanitary and degrading to civilized females. To top all that, no child could withstand such an ordeal for the allotted duration. Therefore it had to be untrue.

The second earthly introduction to the high court was Bishop Fiero Del Este (Iron of the East) of Rome, a tall, robust earth man with reddish brown hair and blue green eyes. He wore elaborate, stately robes with a peaked hat and demonstrated enormous pride in their significance. All of which went ignored at the court of Almira. He was equally tutored and instructed by translators and his defending attorneys. He suffered the ordeal with notable disregard and seemed bored with the proceedings. When asked if he understood the charges, he nodded his head and clearly stated, "I also understand that you have brought the wrong man to trial." And with that said he pompously reclaimed his seat and brought out his prayer beads and commenced to pray, dashing the sign of the cross several times across his chest, convinced his God would see him through this.

The full list of charges against humanity was read to both men who stood in silence before an awesome council. Bishop Fiero del Este with his head still bowed continued to count his prayer beads as if agreeing with the accusations. Anil of Tibet took a long surveying look at his accusers and the assembly of living beings present. The courtroom was enormous and words spoken resonated from the distant walls. All seats were taken and even the balconies surrounding the judicial center were filled to capacity. Many faces strange, different and some even frightening focused on this non-impressive human from prison earth. Whispers rumbled in garbled tones from one individual to another, all of which Anil assumed were aimed at him. Anil of Tibet slowly walked around the courtroom in his calculated stride with his hands behind his back and appeared to be deep in thought. Patiently he surveyed each of the judges and spoke not a word. Having been given the allotted time to respond, he was urged by one of his counselors to answer the charges, the court was waiting and he must not antagonize the judge's patience. Anil of Tibet took a deep breath, placed his hands together on his forehead and bowed ceremoniously to all present in a slow circle. When he finished his seemingly courteous ritual he gathered his hands and lowered them before him. He looked at the presiding individual sitting high in the judge's stand and pleaded loud and clear, "Not Guilty."

Bishop Del Este dropped count of his prayer beads and fumbled to gather the rosary back in order. He then looked at Anil in astonishment that he should rebuke the charges so clearly set out before them and demonstrably true. Man on earth was destroying his own home.

Anil's attorneys called for an immediate conference, severely admonishing Anil of Tibet for his unpredicted plea. He had been instructed to plead guilty as charged and draw a light sentence most likely serving it at one of the civil planets for life. While the guilty humans faced an uncertain future. "Save yourself was the legal advice. There is no hope for mankind on earth. They are guilty of all charges and will most likely be condemned to eternal fire." But, Anil of Tibet would hear none to it. He waved his hands to ward off his defenders and with a bowed head repeated three words constantly. "Let me be. Let … me … be."

Finally the court returned to order, Anil of Tibet was asked to state on what grounds he based his plea? Had he not read in his own earthly language what the charges were? Had his interpreters not made it clear and understandable? Borrowing valor from Anil's behavior Bishop Del Este came to his side and awaited the next episode. Anil commenced his oratory slowly. First answering that he understood the charges perfectly well and that if he were to stumble with his understanding, his interpreters had gained his full confidence and he would call on them to help him move forward and he bowed courteously at his inquisitor. He then waited with his head bowed until he heard the presiding individual say, "Very well. You may proceed."

"I am given to understand that the Wardens of prison earth are equally on trial here. I understand they are held liable for manipulating the incarcerated gene into the creation of the current human form. I wish to state before this court that the Guardians of Death, as they have been called are not guilty as well. They have without doubt proven that intelligence; physical strength and superior technology are not enough to overcome the need to be needed. The need to be admired and even loved, if the word love is still used in your society. They were confined to prison earth as well as the prisoners they guarded. They grew lonesome, if you still allow that sentiment to be accepted. They yearned for company of their own kind and out of boredom experimented with some available toys. It became an experiment that multiplied beyond expectation on a planet hungry for living beings. From a need to be needed the Guardians of Death are guilty of absorbing adoration and allowing that adoration to go uncontrolled. I am given to understand that the Guardians of Death were assigned to prevent the outlaw gene from escaping earth. And they did that very well, none of us have ever left what is now our home. It is said they were granted the power to educate the human breed and they did that very well also. From space dust to a gene, to a man and to earthly dust has been a stupendous journey for mankind. The Guardians of Death fell from grace when they became over indulgent, when they enslaved primitive man to build temples in which the Guardians of Death could be worshipped. The human gene originated from a highly intelligent species such as all of you here. That mankind should wish to progress and become more intelligent is a quest deeply embedded in the original gene. Generations have lived and died and each individual has been an active member of that pursuit. Without the original gene, outlaw or not man would not have progressed to his present state. If the Guardians of Death are guilty of anything else, I do not know it. I state before this court that the Guardians are only guilty of finding love too powerful an elixir to overcome under their living conditions. They were in effect novices in the emotion of loving and being loved. They fell victims to their emotional needs. Should the word emotion, still be allowed to exist in your society? I beg this court to show leniency for these short-comings of the Guardians. Instead of expulsion from the security of your civilization perhaps a long rest period from the turbulence of earth would restore them to their proper directives."

The voice from the judge's stand resounded to shock Anil and the Bishop. "Have the earth men been informed about the human brain fuel cell conspiracy?" And the defending attorneys answered in a loud unified, "No!" It would never be known how much time was granted to further hide the evidence by the distillers of brain power cells with one simple "NO."

When Anil and the Bishop asked their attorneys and interpreters to explain the question, they went silent and refused to speak of it. Instead they emphasized that it was a separate issue with no room for discussion here and now. Furthermore it had nothing to do with their reason for being here and so they closed the discussion.

"You have defended your jailers well, earth man. And the court will consider your suggestions. But you are here charged with a volume of offenses against your kind. The destruction of your prison is not a light charge. Your planet was carefully planned and constructed to self regenerate and you have seriously disrupted that process. Your kind has annihilated countless life forms on your planet and threatens many more. Humans have invaded without regard the inner core of your planet and disrupted safety measures established to provide stability to all surface populations. Man has devastated the resources planned to provide the very air you breathe, the water you drink and the food you eat. How do you plead to that?

"Not guilty!" echoed the reply.

"May, may I intercede here?" A visibly frightened Bishop Del Este stuttered humbly. And he was granted passage. "Rather than castigate the child for his unruly behavior, would it not be more prudent to question the source of the child's unruliness? Mankind in his present state is like a child among you. A team of educators was sent by you to educate man in the ways of justice and social rightness but man was no longer an infant. He was by then a mature living being. Empowered by a gene from his previous existence that overwhelmed his understanding and motivated him to grab food and territory for self security where food was most available. He had acquired a family by then and providing for them was the first priority in his developing mind. Man did not set out to conquer the world by fist and hammer without first being introduced to ungoverned power. It is my concept that in this area the Guardians of Death may have over extended their lessons of behavior. And man did not have the knowledge to set aside what was not right and socially acceptable. Let alone the physical strength to refuse the driving force instilled in him by association with celestial beings. Here should rest due consideration to the frightening power citizens of your society demonstrated to the awe stricken man. Man was a scared child. Man was incapable of harnessing his progress since he knew not the laws of restraint. Men had recently overcome dwelling in hovels and caves and saw the glorious comfort in which the Guardians of Death lived and struggled to achieve a degree of that comfort for themselves. Some will say that I am shifting the blame of man's comportment away from him. When in reality, man had no other source of guidance and he took his lessons well. There were no barriers to progress. No limits, no restrictions to inhibit his forward momentum. As his intelligence grew he came to accept that he was rapidly consuming his own planet. Man is fighting fiercely to overcome the errors of his past. He valiantly seeks to find remedies to his ill use of given lessons. Man can live in comfort without destroying his domain. But first he must learn to better rule himself. And perhaps I may be speaking out of term here, but consider that man has long lived without reins on his comportment. And although religion has been a slow teacher, it is nonetheless an opportunity for man to rise above his abrasive self. The gene that motivates man to believe in something grander than himself is too firmly implanted from his previous existence to remove in a short period of time. The Guardians of Death may well have a grip on the salvation of mankind. I will not deny that as I speak before you, I fear a bolt of lightning may strike me dead, at any moment. Since it appears that we were brought here to tell us our future fate and not to judge our efforts to survive a gruesome penalty. Therefore, I must hold firm to my belief that given the opportunity to overcome his wrongful ways and allowing him to find solutions to his self made dilemma man can be a civil citizen of your society. Mankind is worthy of consideration due to his tenacity to overcome the countless obstacles laid before him. By

whatever means." And the Bishop gave the judges seat an uniden-
tified look then ceremoniously regained his seat and picked up his
prayer beads where he left off.

Anil of Tibet asked if he could speak and so he did. "I no longer know what to call the Guardians of Death. I feel no shame that I
should be confused by the name changes. But leaving the judgment
of the GODs or the VOLS to the better understanding of your
civilization, I have nothing further to say in their defense or their
tenure on earth. I do wish to call the courts attention to countless
stories known among humans that the Wardens of prison earth
fathered innumerable half human half celestial beings. Also some
females of your society gave birth to children sired by humans.
And hushed whispers spread rapidly across the vast courtroom.
And I must question the courts whether these innocent offspring
will be condemned also? Even though they know not what they
have done to deserve punishment. Please, allow me to question by
what sense of justice is this action considered right? I, like Bishop
Del Este fear your wrath. But you brought me here to try me for
the wrong doings of mankind. And I plead not guilty to all charges
for if your rule of law castigates the child for the sins of the father,
then your society requires serious revision. You would penalize me
for the wrong doing of others just as well. Anil's and the Bishop's
attorneys were seen busy rounding up their material as if ready to
end their assignment. The humans had self condemned.

"Each human being like each of you present is a universe unto
themselves and each of us is guilty of our own wrong doing and
deserve merit for our righteous actions. If that is not the case in
your society, then I harbor not a thread of hope for the pre-doomed
human on earth. Annihilation in one swift blow instead of a slow
torturous incarceration would be a far kinder judgment. I will plead
further like Bishop Del Este that should this court decide to grant
the human kind an opportunity to find righteousness through
religion then consider this. Celestial beings have run an obstacle
course of adoration on earth. And that is what brought us to this
point. Perhaps an envoy, a human envoy, a teacher born among

them on the same earth as all men. One that humans can relate to as one of their very own kind would be a wiser effort to bring the laws of righteousness to the unruly human.

"It will no doubt take time to convert man into a civil being, worthy of respect among you. But, investigate man's record closely and you will find an existence worth saving. Man is rightfully your next of kin. I say it is wrong to destroy a child of your making."

The court was called into recess. The presiding judge announced that the council would sit to consider the earth men's declarations and would withhold judgment on mankind, the GODs and the VOLS until a later time.

But time on earth is a devise man invented to measure his life span and record all events within his world. The system coincides with the earth's rotations around the sun. A mechanical occurrence that is dependable and is relied upon for accuracy to an infinite degree. Whereas cosmic time is charged with enormous complexities far beyond man's comprehension. A minute in cosmic time could well be a year on earth. Within that gigantic difference of measure earth men and the citizens of Galaxy 12 stood at enormous odds. By the time the court at Almira reconvened, Anil of Tibet and Bishop Fiero Del Este would be names found only in earth's ancient history books.

Conflicts within the GODs and the VOLS continued for time unkept by the minds of man. It was eons before principled warriors stood supreme over a defeated assembly of wrongful Wardens. Some would stand trial for their transgressions, others were claimed by earth's environmental conditions and still others by the power of greater warriors. The VOLS managed to elude justice in minute numbers and would continue to plague mankind for time immeasurable. Of the righteous former Wardens of planet earth, one stood alone torn and battle scarred but held firm to his given assignment, to reach out and bring man out of wrongful oblivion and into the light of righteousness. His heroics were well documented at the courts of Almira. He was rewarded with supreme immortality. He would never die and He was granted the coded name of YH YH (Yh Yv) by earthly translation.

Celestial beings had long conquered the technology of employing the powerful gravitational pull of black holes in outer space and use that energy to propel their ships at unimaginable speeds. Therefore travel between galaxies was reduced dramatically by earth's standards. A secondary source of energy was in common use by drawing energy from the light produced by stars —Star light is a viable source of power. Solar wind velocity had been harnessed and cosmic radiation was used in far reaches of other galaxies as a reliable propellant.

The startled human passengers only saw full fledged stars, planets and space debris dashing by their portholes without definition for a short time and suddenly they were home in the comfort of their beds and bewildered by the dream they just had.

At a monastery skillfully wedged against a formidable rock cliff and sweeping slopes of green grasses, a young novice monk was serving breakfast to his teacher, Anil of Tibet. He brought a bowl of warm water and fresh towels to wash away Anil's sleep from his eyes. Breakfast was warm yak milk, various cheeses and fresh baked bread with butter and honey, while the delectable aroma of tea helped to wake up the senses. Anil sat upright to look out his window into the vastness and beauty of the Himalayan Mountains. Among the peaks of these mighty mountains the famous God Shiva's head gave birth to the Ganges River. It's the river of life, a dominant force always reliable. Multiple streams contribute to the river's journey to the sea. While on the way "the daughter of the mountains" sustained countless life forms. Already a flock of marsh birds floated silently across a flawless sky to their favorite feeding places and Anil found soul filling joy in the sight. Of all this Anil was an integral part. To know it was his unquestioned home gave him a sense of peace and security, in spite of the frightening dream of last night or moments ago. Beyond the mighty Himalayas the sun was brightening the horizon. Snow covered peaks gave way to vast meadows where goats and yak were led to feed. A warm glow highlighted the panorama and a morning breeze filled the air with the exhilarating joy of life. The lacebark pines were gently swaying in the breeze that always swept their limbs in the early mornings. He harbored the need to speak of his dream and felt foolish to do so. Instead he looked again out his window as if seeking guidance and was greeted by a flawless sky painted in a shade of blue so beautiful; he could only call it heavenly. And knew in his heart it was sent to him by a heavenly power. Suddenly, he felt strangely happy and asked the novice monk to sit and visit with him for a while. "I had the most bizarre dream last night. I dreamed I was in a strange court of law defending myself against the follies of mankind. Somehow I knew I left earth only an instant ago and suddenly I arrived at this very strange court room. I was accused of creating all the harm the earth has suffered since the beginning of humanity. My accusers were a fearsome race I have never seen before and honestly don't want to see again. I pleaded not guilty to all charges since I feel certain that celestial intervention altered the course of human history on earth. I struggled to cast aside my fears and spoke to a strange tribunal to that effect for a long time. I was also defending a God but, I don't remember which God and for what. I feared for my life every second I was there. But, I refused to be intimidated, somehow knowing they would not kill me. I also remember flashing past countless stars to an unknown destination. Then everything went blank and I woke up. It was only a dream. But a dream so real, it was terrifying."

The young monk listened politely then as if anxious to go to his other assignments gently stated, "I have learned in this place that dreams always have a thread of truth within each one. Perhaps the Gods are conveying a message to you." The young monk concluded picking up the breakfast dishes and left to serve other monks their first meal.

An assistant warden having served on the scientific staff during his tenure on earth was restored to his home planet beyond Galaxy 12. Having served His commission honorably and been instrumental in defeating the Vols was rewarded with an enormous promotion and time to readjust to a new role of life on the civil planets of Voltimar. They were admirable beings of graceful limb and slender bodies. Their physiques resonated of athletic activity, muscular and yet not bulky. The color of their skin was a mellow gold on the edge of being ivory and they glowed as if lit from within. They seemed to float across the floor rather than walk. In all they did, they reflected awesome physical strength in an effortless fluid fashion. They dwelled in ease and comfort on a sterile planet free of illness or life ending threats. Order reigned supreme here and to disrupt the peace was unthinkable. By mutual agreement his life mate and himself requested permission to become parents of a male child and accepted responsibility for another living being. After a shortened waiting period their case was honored and granted license to submit their reproductive fluids to a predestined birth laboratory. Their contribution to a new life was cared for to the infinite degree. The mother was spared the burden of carrying a child within her body for the prescribed time. All the care required for a healthy and disease free infant was a matter of routine. As the embryo developed, educational programs were transmitted to the child's brain. Upon the parent's request their child could receive multiple instructions on any given subject. Be it music, the arts, politics, galaxy geography or any other subject the parents chose. From these educational programs, the grown child could select which was best suited to them.

Their offspring was now in its third growing phase as friends and relatives gathered to celebrate the child's progress. No element of festivity was ignored and all attendants presented their gifts and well wishes as a customary ritual. Enjoying the attention as any child his age would do, he brought gasps of surprise when he announced before everybody that "he could remember having lived on a small planet called earth." The child's educational programs were progressing admirably so it came as no surprise the child could speak so well. He further startled his listeners by stating that he also remembered "riding into an ancient community on a strange beast of a faded color and that people cheered him as he went by. And in my previous life my father's name was Joseph and my mother was Mary."

Only the male parent, once a renowned warrior understood that before him was a "Source Of Unexplained Life" such as he investigated while on the scientific staff on earth. His son was a "soul" that found a way to escape the surly bonds of earth to dwell in peace and harmony on the civil planets of Voltimar. No doubt a great place to recuperate. Perhaps at a future time, he would urge the supreme council to consider sending his son to earth as an envoy. Perhaps as a long awaited messenger of high regard to cure the ills of men and bring new light to his troubled existence.

The End ?